LEVI STRAUSS
gets a BRIGHT IDEA

A Fairly Fabricated Story of a Pair of Pants

Written by Tony Johnston

Illustrated by Stacy Innerst

HARCOURT CHILDREN'S BOOKS
Houghton Mifflin Harcourt
Boston   New York   2011

Harcourt Children's Books is an imprint of
Houghton Mifflin Harcourt Publishing Company.

www.hmhbooks.com

The illustrations in this book were done in acrylic on blue jeans.
The text type was set in Slab American.
The display type was set in Roadkill.
Design by Regina Roff

Library of Congress Cataloging-in-Publication Data

Johnston, Tony, 1942-
Levi Strauss gets a bright idea or : a fairly fabricated story of a pair of pants /
written by Tony Johnston ; illustrated by Stacy Innerst.
p. cm.
Summary: Retells, in tall-tale fashion, how Levi Strauss went to California during the
Gold Rush, saw the need for a sturdier kind of trousers, and invented jeans.
ISBN 978-0-15-206145-6
1. Strauss, Levi, 1829-1902—Juvenile fiction. {1. Strauss, Levi, 1829-1902—Fiction.
2. Jeans (Clothing) —Fiction. 3. Clothing and dress—Fiction. 4. Gold mines and
mining—California—Fiction. 5. California—History—1850-1950—Fiction.
6. Tall tales.} I. Innerst, Stacy, ill. II. Title.
PZ7.J6478Lev 2011
{E}—dc22
2010043402

Manufactured in China
LEO 10 9 8 7 6 5 4 3 2 1
4500289774

For Jeannette Larson, who got the bright idea,
for Roger Johnston, who reviles all jeans but Levi's,
and for Levi Spalter, who bears an excellent name —T.J.

For Stuart, Olivia, and Jake —S.I.

"GOLD!"

somebody yelled. Next thing anybody knew, the whole world **rushed to California** and started digging up the place. The trouble was, they rushed so fast, **they lost their pants.**

Well, they didn't exactly lose them. The pants just **disintegrated**. They were *that* flimsy. Corduroy, wool, tweed, flannel, burlap, velvet, worsted, serge: they didn't last long in the gold fields. Right quick they got worked down to the size of a handkerchief.

Soon, every miner was sluicing for color in his **long johns**— or naked as a jaybird. Yessir, all of California was mining in the vanilla.

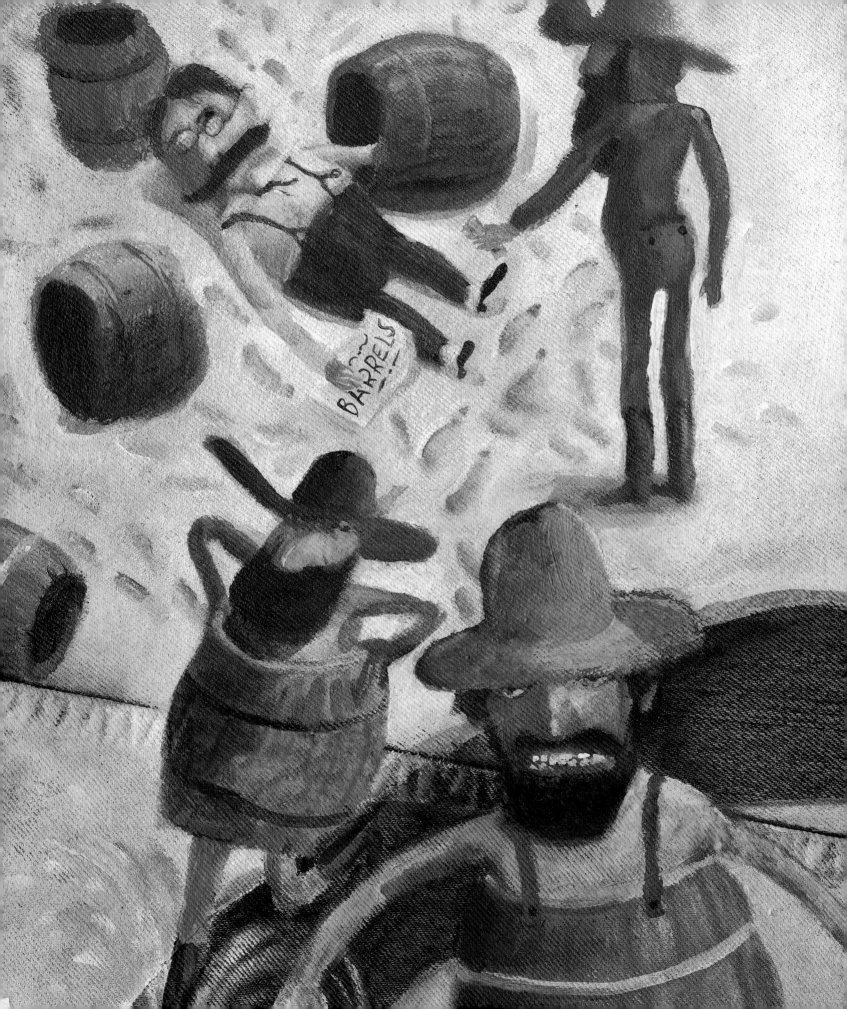

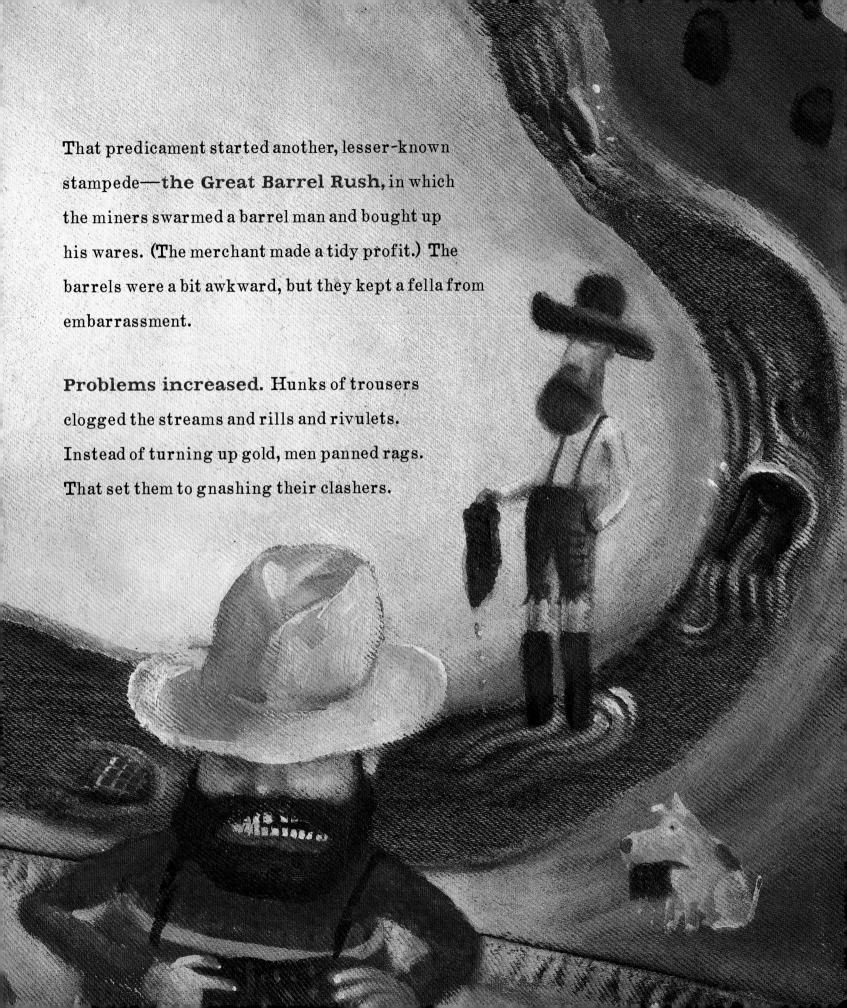

That predicament started another, lesser-known stampede—**the Great Barrel Rush,** in which the miners swarmed a barrel man and bought up his wares. (The merchant made a tidy profit.) The barrels were a bit awkward, but they kept a fella from embarrassment.

Problems increased. Hunks of trousers clogged the streams and rills and rivulets. Instead of turning up gold, men panned **rags.** That set them to gnashing their clashers.

At that very time, Levi Strauss rushed west from New York City.

He rushed slowly, so he came late and missed the gold.

"DANG!" said Levi Strauss.

He looked around and scratched his beard. "Hmmmm," he said.

"There's a need for something here. I wonder what?"

One day when Levi Strauss was gazing at the be-barreled men, **a light lit up** in his brain.

"DANG!" said Levi Strauss. "These men need pants that last."

Levi Strauss was slick with a needle and scissors. He set out to build a better trouser. He tinkered with tree bark. He tinkered with blankets. He even tinkered with quilts. But Levi Strauss was not satisfied with the results.

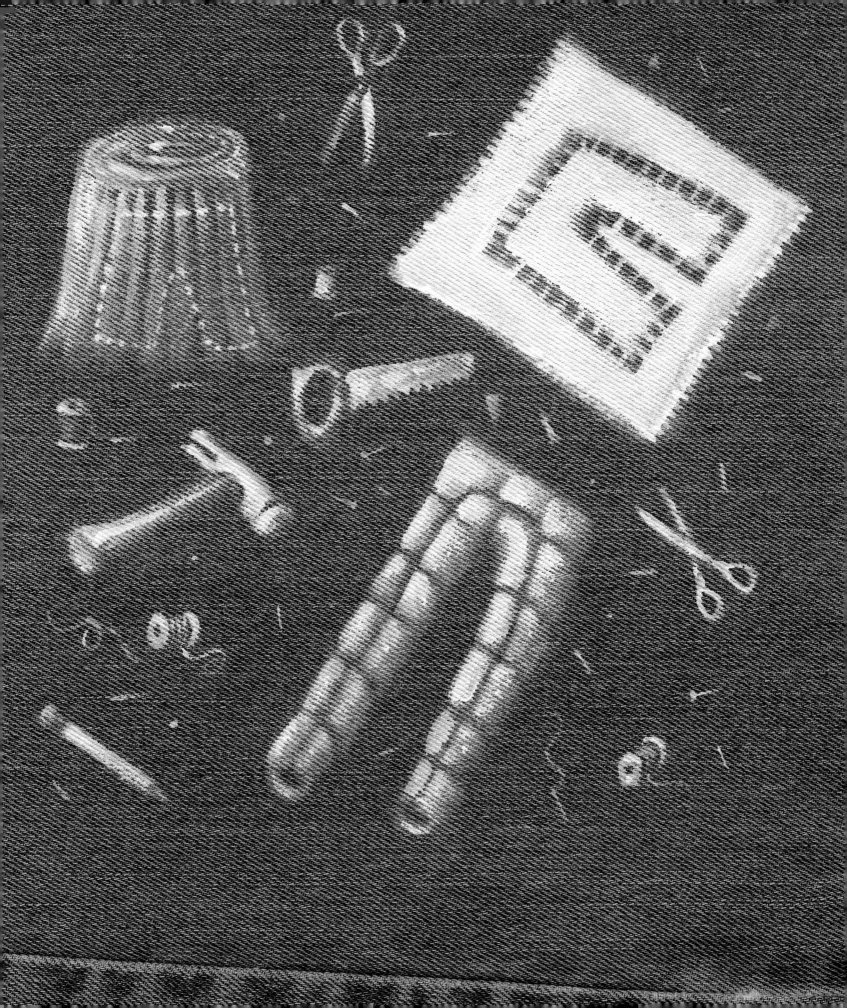

Meanwhile, he sewed tents to keep the miners safe from the elements.

A man wearing nothing more than a barrel
got pretty hot when the sun sizzled,

pretty cold when it snowed.

Those tents were tough as buffalo hides. Neither sun nor wind nor snow nor sleet nor hail nor rain was any match for them.

Levi Strauss's brain lit up. **"DANG!"** he shouted. "That's it! Tents!"
In no time he clipped his own tent to bits and spliced it together as—

PANTS!

Right off he put them to a test. He hitched a horse to each trouser leg and hollered, "PULL!" Did the pants tear in two? Nope. Not a single thread popped.

"DANG!" said Levi Strauss. He pulled those tent-pants on.

Don't think the miners weren't watching.

Intent on having those pants, they roared like an earthquake, "AFTER HIM!" Another dash was on—the Great Pants Rush.

Levi Strauss rushed away. The miners barreled right behind, rattling and racketing and rolling. But they were no match for the nimble Strauss in his indestructible tent-pants.

Though he was dexterous, Levi Strauss knew he couldn't outfit every soul in California. He wasn't *that* nimble with a needle. So he sent for his brothers. They rushed from New York City (with their needles) to assist.

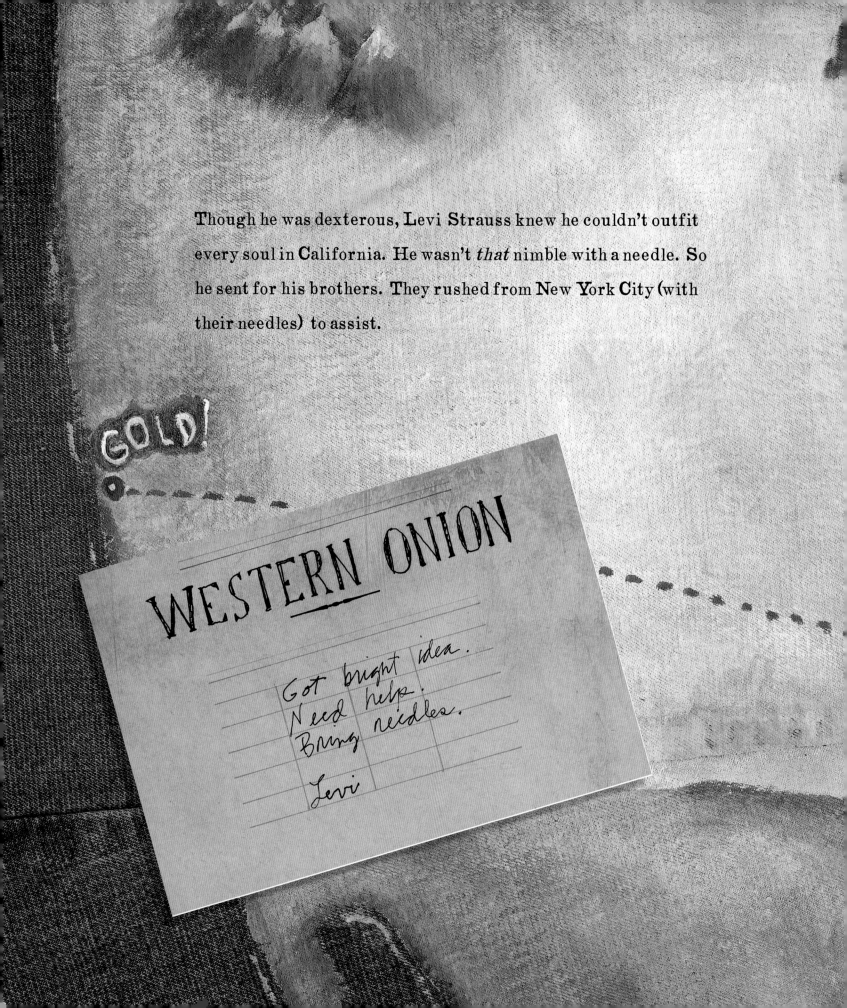

Pretty soon, each miner had a spanking new pair of tent-pants. Then weren't they just beside themselves! In comfort, they sluiced and panned and rocked their cradles for the bright yellow stuff. They rushed, rushed, **RUSHED**. No harm came to those pants.

They were so overcome with gratitude,
the men named their new gear after **Levi** himself.

"DANG!" said Levi Strauss.

He blushed.

Just when things were going real well, a further problem reared its head. The miners cherished their new pants so, they refused to take them off. Even for baths. The whole of California stank like cheese ripening in the sun.

"Hmmmm," said Levi Strauss. "There's a need for something here. I wonder what?"

His brain lit up again. Levi Strauss cried, "Two are better than one!"

The Strauss brothers set to. Their needles flashed so fast, they nearly melted. Soon, every miner owned a pair of pants—and a spare.

Those men would have elected Levi Strauss president. But he just wanted to sew. He was content with that.

Instead of the presidency, Levi Strauss ended up with a mountain of barrels. He scratched his beard. "Hmmmm," he said. "There's a use for these. **I wonder what?**"

One day he was pondering that when his brain lit up.

"DANG!" said Levi Strauss. He snatched up a hammer and rushed into the streets.

And in no time, don't you know, from that passel of barrels Levi Strauss built the city of **San Francisco**.

DANG!

The story of Levi Strauss and the invention of blue jeans is mostly legend with threads of truth, which my version stretches to near popping.

Levi Strauss came from Germany to the United States in 1847. In New York City, he and his brothers sold all sorts of stuff to people who needed all sorts of stuff. After somebody shouted "GOLD!," he and his stuff—including tough canvas for wagon covers and tents—went west to where the shout came from: San Francisco. The gold rush started in 1848, but Levi didn't make it to California till 1853. He realized right off that there was more money to be made selling stuff to gold grubbers than in mining gold himself. So Levi had the Strauss boys back east send him more stuff to peddle. (His brothers were a big help, but they didn't rush to the gold fields with their needles.) Levi peddled so much, they all got rich.

Miners in California didn't exactly pan for gold clad in barrels or in the vanilla (their birthday suits), but their pants were pretty raggedy. So threadbare, in fact, that gold dust sometimes sifted out of holes in their pockets. They *really* needed somebody to invent invincible pants. But whoever first made the tent-canvas pants Levi sold is a mystery.

Levi Strauss may not have sewn any blue jeans, but he sure made them famous. He was helped by Jacob Davis, a Latvian tailor who joined the pants-making outfit. Jacob added orange stitching and copper rivets, eleven in all, to the weakest spots, like the corners of pockets. His rivet brain wave was so good, Davis decided to patent it. But he needed a partner. Levi knew a bright idea when he saw one and stepped in. In 1873, jeans as we know them were born.

Levi Strauss helped the city of San Francisco by giving bundles of money for charity and education. He was so beloved, flags flew at half-mast when he died in 1902. What a guy! Somebody called him "one of the potent factors in building the city." But building the city from barrels—well, that's a pure-dee fabrication.